It Looked
Like Spilt Milk

by Charles G. Shaw

HarperCollinsPublishers

IT LOOKED LIKE SPILT MILK

Copyright, 1947, by Charles G. Shaw

ISBN 0-06-025566-8
ISBN 0-06-025565-X (lib. bdg.)
ISBN 0-06-443159-2 (pbk.)
L.C. Card 47-30767

Sometimes it looked
like Spilt Milk.
But it wasn't Spilt Milk.

Sometimes it looked

like a Rabbit.

But it wasn't a Rabbit.

Sometimes it looked

like a Bird.

But it wasn't a Bird.

Sometimes it looked

like a Tree.

But it wasn't a Tree.

Sometimes it looked
   like an Ice Cream Cone.
But it wasn't an Ice Cream Cone.

Sometimes it looked

like a Flower.

But it wasn't a Flower.

Sometimes it looked
like a Pig.
But it wasn't a Pig.

Sometimes it looked
like a Birthday Cake.
But it wasn't a Birthday Cake.

Sometimes it looked

like a Sheep.

But it wasn't a Sheep.

Sometimes it looked
like a Great Horned Owl.
But it wasn't a Great Horned Owl.

Sometimes it looked

like a Mitten.

But it wasn't a Mitten.

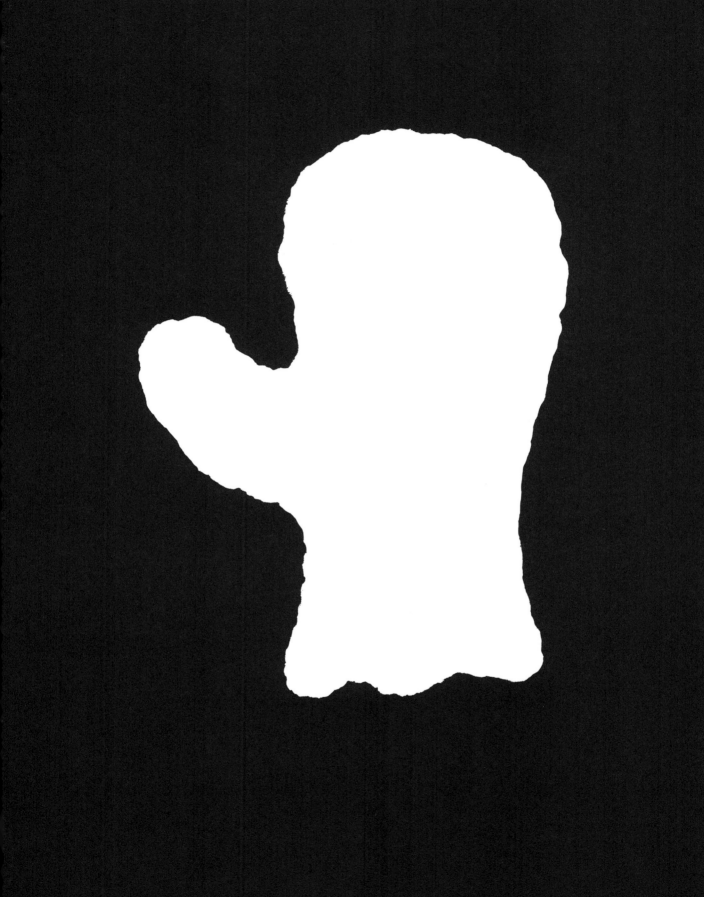

Sometimes it looked
like a Squirrel.
But it wasn't a Squirrel.

Sometimes it looked

like an Angel.

But it wasn't an Angel.

Sometimes it looked
like Spilt Milk.
But it wasn't Spilt Milk.

It was just a Cloud in the Sky.